a story for small bear

To Ashley Beitel, PhD, author of the parenting
book *Childproofing for Adolescence.*
You knew there was a story to tell. —A.B.M.

For Dad —R.J.

Text copyright © 2020 by Alice B. McGinty
Jacket art and interior illustrations copyright © 2020 by Richard Jones

All rights reserved. Published in the United States by Schwartz & Wade Books, an imprint of Random House Children's Books,
a division of Penguin Random House LLC, New York.

Schwartz & Wade Books and the colophon are trademarks of Penguin Random House LLC.

Visit us on the Web! rhcbooks.com

Educators and librarians, for a variety of teaching tools, visit us at RHTeachersLibrarians.com

Library of Congress Cataloging-in-Publication Data is available upon request.
ISBN 978-1-9848-5227-4 (hc)
ISBN 978-1-9848-5228-1 (glb)
ISBN 978-1-9848-5229-8 (ebook)

ISBN 978-0-593-38017-8 (proprietary edition)

The text of this book is set in 19-point Belen.
The illustrations were rendered in acrylic and watercolor paint and edited in Adobe Photoshop.
Book design by Rachael Cole

MANUFACTURED IN CHINA
10 9 8 7 6 5 4 3

This Imagination Library edition is published by Random House Children's Books, a division of Penguin Random
House, exclusively for Dolly Parton's Imagination Library, a not-for-profit program designed to inspire a love of
reading and learning, sponsored in part by The Dollywood Foundation. Penguin Random House's trade editions
of this work are available wherever books are sold.

a story for
small bear

written by **Alice B. McGinty**
illustrated by **Richard Jones**

schwartz & wade books · new york

When a late-autumn wind
swirled into their den after noontime nap,
Small Bear shivered. *Brrrrr.*

"I smell frost in the air," Mama said.
"Tonight we'll start our winter slumber."

Small Bear snuggled close.

"Will you tell me stories before we sleep?" she asked.

"I'd love that," Mama said.
"But there's work to finish first.
If you help—
no dilly, no dally—
then we'll have time for stories."

Small Bear got right to work.
With the sun shining high,
she helped Mama gather sprigs of spruce
to make a soft, warm nest.

As Small Bear raked the forest floor,
she came upon her favorite spot—
the cozy hole in the spruce tree.

She rubbed her nose in the sweet-smelling wood. *Mmm!*

She scratched her back. *Ahh!*

She could dilly and dally here forever.

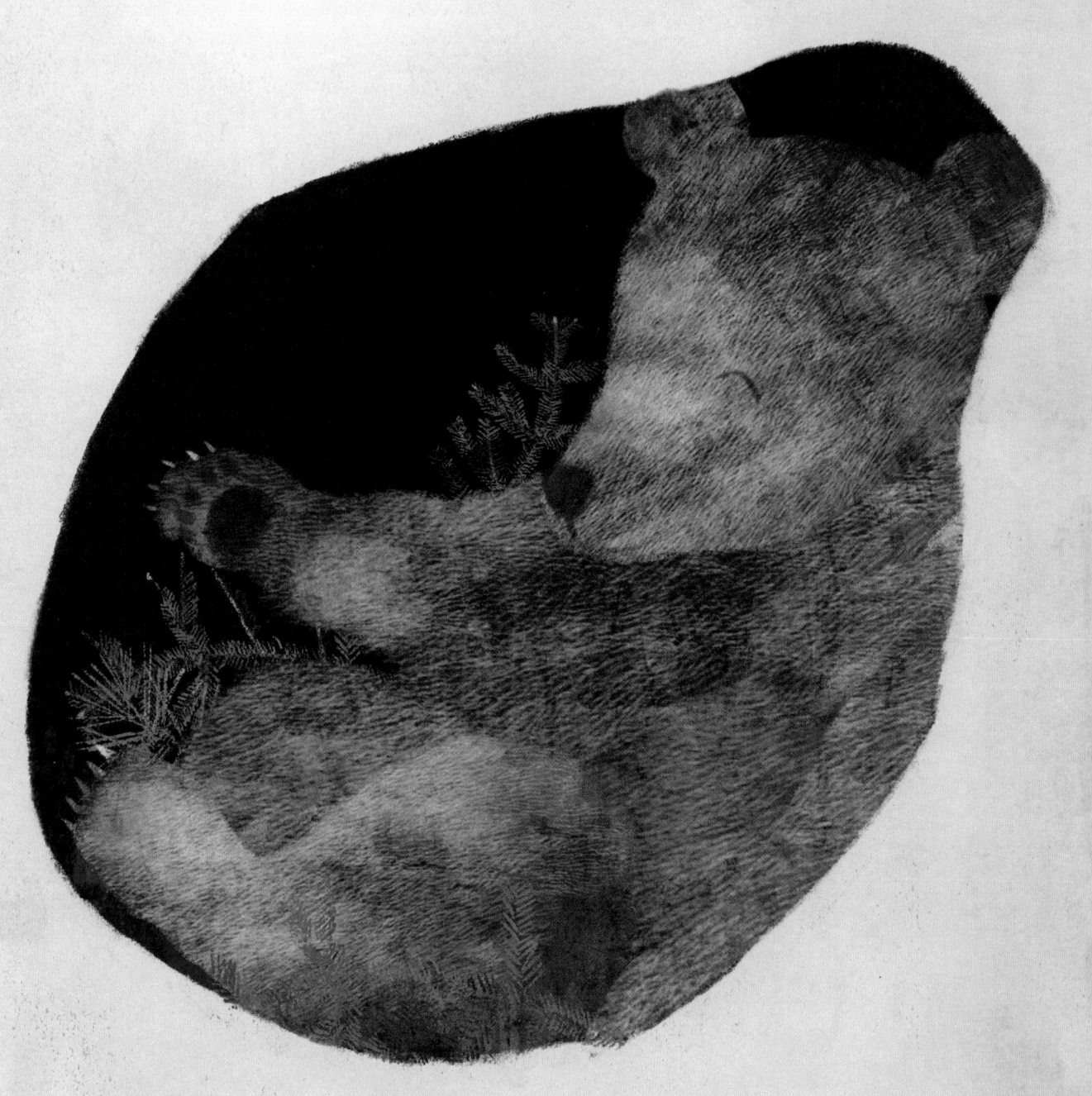

But then a gust of frigid air ruffled her fur
and Small Bear shuddered.
She did not like cold. Not at all.

Small Bear thought of Mama nearby.
"No dilly," she told herself. "No dally."
Wind was biting,
winter knocking,
and she had to save time for stories.

"Goodbye, hole," said Small Bear,
and she carried the sprigs back
to line her winter bed.

As the sun drifted slowly across the sky,
Small Bear and Mama lumbered to the river to bathe.

Small Bear tumbled into the clear, cool water
and shimmied until all the dirt had been washed from her fur. *Ahh!*
She splished and splashed. *Mmm!*

No dilly.

She knew that's what Mama would say.

Still, she rolled and wriggled and played some more.

No dally, Small Bear thought.

But it was so hard to leave!

What could she do?
Wind was biting,
winter knocking,
and she had to save time for stories.
Finally, firmly, Small Bear waded to shore.

"Goodbye, river," she said,
and shook herself dry.

"Mama!" Small Bear called.

"Where are you, Mama?"

At last, Small Bear saw her

and ran to meet her by the berry grove.

Late-day sunshine warmed them
as they munched on berries, juicy and red.
Then Small Bear saw acorns
high above.

Up, up, up she climbed,
one branch to another,
and ate acorn
after acorn. *Mmm!*
She looked out
from the branches. *Ahh!*
She could climb forever.

But now the sun began to curve into sunset.

"No dilly," Small Bear reminded herself.

Still, she reached for a particularly plump acorn.

"No dally," Small Bear said.

But how could she leave?

The forest was full of food and adventure.

Suddenly, though, Small Bear shivered. *Brrrrr.*

Sun was setting,

wind was biting,

winter knocking,

and she *had* to save time for stories.

Small Bear knew what to do.
"Goodbye, trees," she said,
and down she scrambled.

"Mama!" she called.

She scampered between bushes,

scurried over rocks.

"Mama! Mama!"

Finally, Small Bear saw her
lumbering near the mulberry trees.
"Here I am, Mama!" she said.

And together, they started down the path toward home.

Back in their den,

warm and clean and fed,

Small Bear and her mama

nestled down into their spruce-bough nest.

"Did I save enough time for stories?"

Small Bear asked.

"You did," Mama answered, and pulled her close.

In a deep, rumbling voice,
Mama began.
"Once there lived a small bear
who loved to play.

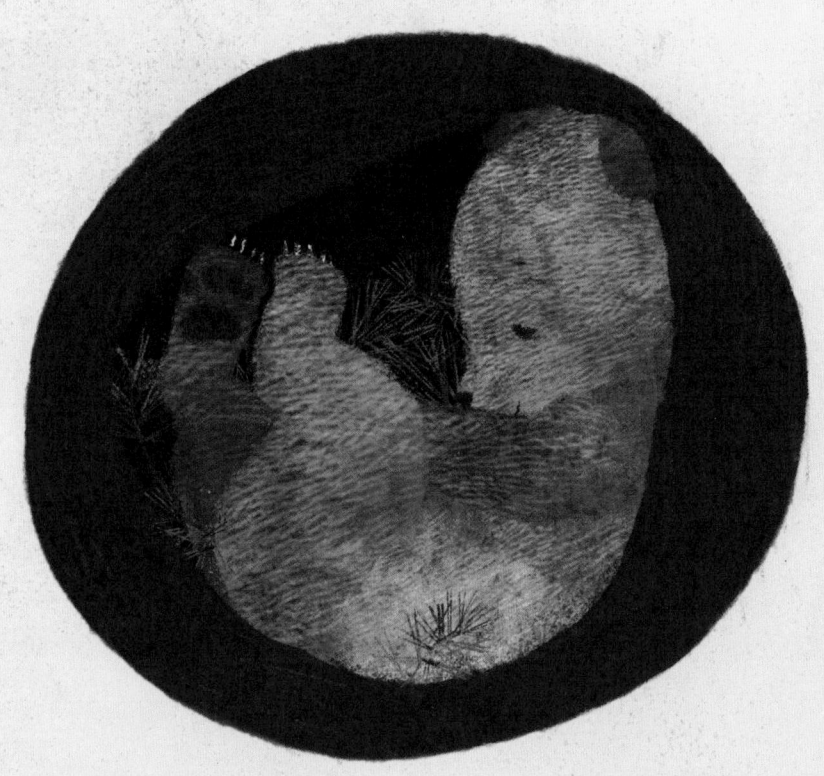

Her mama watched
as she scratched in her cozy hole—
no dilly—

splashed in her clear, cool stream—
no dally—

and adventured in the tall, tall trees.
Would she save time for stories?"

Small Bear listened,
content,
because she knew
how this story would end.

And as the first snowflakes of winter
floated down outside,
she drifted off to sleep.